I0654015

First Edition.

No. 272—Thrilling Life Stories for the Masses—One Penny.

Whom the Queen delighteth to Honor.

By Birdye Latham Hartland

THRILLING STORIES' COMMITTEE, MANCHESTER.

Gordon & Gotch (London), Agents for Perth, Western Australia, Melbourne, Sydney and Cape Town.

Whom the Queen Honors

By BIRDYE L. HARTLAND

Part 3 of the Shamrock Romances

Edited by Eva Valentine

WHOM THE QUEEN HONORS
Originally published in 1900 by Thrilling Stories Committee and Birdye Latham
Hartland
Copyright © 2020 by Eva Valentine

All rights reserved. Published in the United States by Victorian Workhouse Press. No part of this book may be used or reproduced in any manner whatsoever without written permission from the publisher except in the case of brief quotations embodied in critical articles or reviews; nor may any part of this book be reproduced, stored in a retrieval system, or transmitted in any form or by any means – electronic, mechanical, photocopying, recording, alien transfer, ESP, or other – without written permission from the publisher.
The information in this book is true and complete to the best of our knowledge at proof time. Although the author has made every effort to ensure that the information in the book was correct at press time, the author does not assume and hereby disclaims any liability to any part for any loss, damage, or disruption caused by errors or omissions, whether such errors or omissions result from scheming landlords, scandalized vicars, hysterical heiresses, morbid charladies, rascally youths, murderous magistrates, crazed cats, plague!!!, or any other cause.
P.S. Wear a mask! Wash your hands! <3

Ordering information: For details, contact the publisher at
victorianworkhousepress@gmail.com
Cover design by Black Widow Covers

ISBN: 978-1-953196-39-2

First Edition: January 2020

10 9 8 7 6 5 4 3 2 1 blast off!

Find all of the Shamrock Romances – and even more
good old Victorian novels – on our Tumblr page!

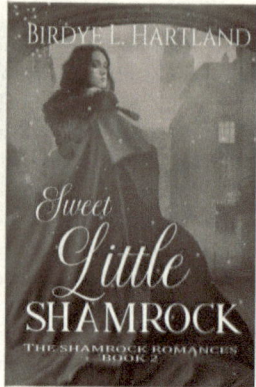

Table of Contents

Editor's Note

Whom the Queen Honors, originally titled *Whom the Queen Delighteth to Honor,* as well as all the other books in this series, was originally published in 1900 as a penny novel – a type of serialized novel that was published weekly as a cheap magazine that cost, of course, only a penny. These serialized novels came to be called penny dreadfuls, simply because the quality of the writing just ... wasn't the best. But people loved reading them, so it's cool.

I am a sucker for old books. When I was in high school, I read Victorian novels by the truckload. I got started on an old copy of *St. Elmo* that my grandpa had picked up at an auction, and read some of my books that my great-grandma had (I still have her old copy of *The Masquerader* by Katherine Cecil Thurston), and picked up many more via interlibrary loan. It's a love that still continues today.

I've been writing books for a long time, but I also love finding old books and editing them to bring them to a new audience. And that's what I'm doing with these old penny novels. I'm transcribing them and editing them to bring them to the readers once more. These old stories are in the public domain, no longer under copyright, so anybody can do what they like with these old stories.

On one hand, it would be a lot easier to simply transcribe these stories and throw them out into the world, the way a lot of internet marketers are doing with books in the public domain. There are half a million (this is a very rough estimate) copies of *Pride and Prejudice* or *Anne of Green Gables* on Amazon. It's a very popular thing right now for internet marketers to grab a copy of the book off Project Gutenberg, convert it into an ebook, and threw it onto Amazon with the other half-million editions that internet marketers are throwing out there. A lot of people are going after the "passive marketing" of using public domain content and earning money from it.

I'm publishing these little books more out of love for those old stories, and because bringing these old books back to life is something of a fun craft project for me. I see stuff in the text that needs to be fixed, and I start fixing it, and the next thing I know, hours have passed and I'm sharpening the character motivation in Chapter IX. I spend hours cleaning up the text, which is a mess, then searching for illustrations and building the book and proofreading the pages and getting a pretty cover for it. And then I have a neat little book with a good story in it, ready to go.

It's kind of a fun little gig, to be honest.

General Notes on Editing

Fond she was of the inverted style of sentence, so common in Victorian writing. "Well she knew no sympathy had he for all her misery" is one example of this style of recursive writing which pervaded this story.

These days, authors and readers prize simple sentences that cut quickly to the heart of the matter, instead of these sweet convolutions. The Victorian style called for a gentler, more flowery style of writing, which lend a grand, sonorous sound to the words, and make every moment seem epic. They also loved what today's writers would sneeringly call sentimentality – the teary-eyed, beautiful heroine struggling against a cruel world that did not understand her secret heart, that maligned her even as she strove to stay pure-hearted, raising her eyes to God, who alone heard her secret prayers.

At any rate, while editing this book, I gently straightened some sentences that needed it. Our dear author (or perhaps her editor) apparently had a comma gun that they'd shoot at random into the text, because I must have excised half a million commas out of this book. British Victorian style also uses semicolons heavily; I removed them and tidied up the sentences if they weren't necessary.

I added to the story in places here and there to heighten the tension, or to continue plot elements that the author dropped, or to add some details or a few lines to better explain the characters' motivations. I also added period details, reading old newspaper articles about the role that Ireland played in the South Boer War (though I have Opinions about the lousy role that the English played in colonizing South Africa).

I also added in a little bit about the attack that Charlie wrote about in one of his letters, because when I was reading the original text, I was so aghast at this boneheaded move by the British generals, to fling thousands of their troops into the cannon's mouth in this way, that I had to ascertain that it was true.

Seeking Information About Birdye L. Hartland!

I have been trying to find out anything about her, but to no avail. I've searched the British Library, Google Books, Ancestry, FamilySearch, Google, Newspapers.com, and other sites, using different variants of Birdye's name and switching up searches. I thought that, because she had these stories published, that I would at least pull up a few hits, but to my complete surprise, there has been nothing.

Now, I've done genealogical research and historical research with some hard-to-track women, and generally I've been able to find at least a few nuggets of information about them through one of these methods. I'm a little dismayed that I have not had any luck.

What's more surprising, to me, is that when you have a name with a unique spelling, such as Birdye, it's more likely to come up on genealogical sites. Not in this case!

I will keep searching for Birdye, even after I publish these books. Birdye deserves to have some credit for her work all these years later.

At any rate, if any of you readers have any information about poor Birdye, do please send it along to me at victorianworkhousepress@gmail.com and I'll do the follow-up research and pop it directly into these books.

I do hope you enjoy this book. I plan to release these serials monthly, so follow me on Twitter as @VictorianReader or on Tumbler!

Be sure to buy these books, and tell your friends to buy them too, because at this time I am locked in a garret in some Victorian slum by an evil taskmaster and I'm not allowed to come out until I've edited and published about 56 of these books. Send bread.

All best wishes,
Eva Valentine, editor
Victorian Workhouse Press

CHAPTER I

I know that the Hand is guiding me
Through the shadow to the light,
And I know that all betiding me
Is meted out aright;
I know that the thorny path I tread
Is ruled with a golden line,
And I know that the darker life's tangled thread,
The brighter the rich design.
      -- Frances R. Havergal.

ON and on Dewla went on her flight into the dark city, pausing now and again to be sure that she had not missed her way, for, because the shops were closed, the town looked different, making it more difficult for her to find her way.

Her heart pounded in her ears. She seldom had ventured into the city, for the commotion from all the cabs and horses in the streets still frightened her, and the smoke and soot that hung over the gaslights made it hard to see very far in front of her, especially now at night.

What if she should lose her way in this heartless, noisy city? What if some drunken man came lurching after her? Where was she to go, and where would she sleep once she got there – if she could even find her way?

She had walked only a short distance in the city, mostly to her friend's house and back home. Now she was cut adrift in this city, all because Hugh, her dear husband of only a few months, clearly loved his childhood friend Bella more than he loved Dewla. And his mother and three daughters were all so cruel to her, endlessly heaping scorn on her head until she could no longer bear it.

A nameless terror seized her now. She was too frightened to run, too fearful to stand still.

What is to become of me now? Was her anguished thought as she passed her hand over her face. What is going to happen to me?

Just then, in her distress, the distant sound of music caught her attention. As she drew nearer, she found that it was drifting from an open window close to the deserted thoroughfare. The voice of the singer was rich and sweet.

Dewla hesitated for a moment, still afraid to stop on the street, and she still had a train to catch, but the music was so sweet that she finally paused to listen.

Forgetful of the deepening gloom of eventide and the fast-flying moments, Dewla Smith stood beside the open window, listening to the words of the sweet hymn. Even after the last notes had died away, she did not stir. Tears stood in her eyes, for the music seemed a message of comfort sent for her – her alone.

A white-haired lady sitting in the recess of the bay window was watching, with much interest, the expressive face of the solitary listener outside. Now she rose from her chair, and came close to where Dewla stood.

"Will you not come inside for a moment?" she said, pleasantly. "The wind is sharp, and you look tired."

Dewla started as though awakened from a dream, and the color rose to her cheeks.

"I am in a hurry," Dewla began, forgetting how long she had tarried, listening to the music.

The lady, still watching her with grave, kindly eyes, wondered who this sad-eyed girl could possibly be that the hymn had evidently touched so deeply, wandering alone thus, with night closing in.

"Come in just a moment, dear," she said, winningly. Without waiting for a second refusal, she opened the front door and drew Dewla in.

"You do look weary," she went on, placing a chair to the fire. "Will you not rest for a time, and Martha shall sing again for you?"

"I need to keep going," Dewla said, but their kindness seemed such a luxury to her parched heart, easing her deep loneliness. She didn't want to leave.

The girl at the piano rose and slipped from the room, returning presently with a cup of tea, hot and steaming.

"How kind you both are," murmured Dewla, looking from one to the other in grateful surprise, hearing the familiar lilt and accent in the white-haired woman's words. "Your way of speaking reminds me of my old home, for I am from Ireland."

The white-haired lady smiled. "Well, I am Irish myself, dear," she returned, "and you look chilled through."

Dewla stretched out her hand. It was such a balm to her lonely heart to meet with someone from her own dear country. The stranger took the small, well-gloved fingers between her own.

"I wish I had known you before," faltered Dewla. "It is too late now, because I am going away. In fact, I was on my way to the station, when the sound of music made me stop and listen. Oh, the words were so beautiful."

The elder lady glanced at the small, silver-mounted bag, which Dewla had laid aside on entering. "Where are you going, dear?" she asked, gently, in no tone of curiosity.

Dewla sighed. "I think I shall go to Manchester," she answered, uncertain.

"I suppose you have friends there?"

Dewla shook her head. "No. There is no one there whom I know personally."

"You are accustomed, perhaps, to travelling alone?" The question was asked in some doubt.

"I have never been anywhere by myself – never before – and it seems so strange." She stopped, and her lips quivered.

The white-haired lady still watched her wonderingly. "I feel a little anxious on your account," she said, touching the girl's arm. "Manchester is a large city, and, remember, England is not Ireland."

A frightened look stole into Dewla's dark eyes. "I am wishing to see the editor of one of the magazines published there. I thought I could stay for a few nights at one of the hotels, until – until I knew about the future."

She said the words with so much pathetic sadness, that her listeners were deeply moved.

"Could she not stay at one of our institutes?" inquired the daughter.

To Dewla she added, "There are homes like this in Manchester, and if you would like to stay at one, I can give you a letter of introduction to the lady-superintendent."

Dewla's face brightened. "Oh! It is kind of you," she cried in her old, impulsive way. "And just when I felt so wretchedly lonely and miserable. Surely, God did lead me here, this evening, to hear the lilting words of that beautiful song, and to have you direct me to a place of shelter. I feel that I cannot thank Him, and you, enough."

"I only wish you could remain with us a little longer," the elder lady replied, earnestly. "Are you quite sure that you cannot?"

Dewla hesitated, then shook her head sadly. "I had better not delay," she said, half to herself. "Do you know when the next train leaves for Manchester?"

"In about an hour. There is just time for me to write a line, which will make it all right for you at the 'Eliot Home.' Take a cab at the station, and drive direct there."

"I wish I had known you both before," cried Dewla again, as she watched her new friend take up her pen. "I often felt so very lonely here, and longed for someone who would understand and help me a little."

"Perhaps you have been in a situation?" ventured the younger of the two ladies.

"Oh, no!" and the hot color rose guiltily to Dewla's fair brow. "I have been staying with – relations."

"Still, it wasn't quite like home, was it?" smiled the other, wondering all the while what the secret trouble could have been that made the girl's eyes look so sad.

"No! Not at all." Dewla bent her head to hide her face.

"Ah, my child, there is no place like home, sweet home," observed the white-haired woman, busy with her letter. "What can compensate for a parent's love?"

"Both of my parents are dead," faltered Dewla with a sudden rush of tears as she thought of that dear father, who she had loved so well, in the old happy days at Claisín.

"Poor child!" murmured the other, in low, sympathetic voice. "Truly, the world must oftentimes seem lonely and drear. No wonder that there is a wistful look about your face; it struck me from the first."

Dewla sipped her tea, the kindness of the stranger threatening to bring new tears to her eyes. Why could not Hugh's mother and sisters have shown even a fraction of this kindness to her when she had come to their house, a stranger? How hard would it have been? She covered her eyes.

The white-haired lady finished writing. "If you ever do return to the Potteries, you will not forget to look us up?" she continued, folding the little note. "Martha and I will be only too pleased to welcome you."

Dewla rose to depart, her face and voice full of thankful gratitude. "If I return, it will be a pleasure to stop by and see you."

"The station is but a little way, and it is straight down this street, so you needn't worry about losing your way. You need not hurry; there is plenty of time yet. Good-bye, my dear, and I am truly glad to be of any little service. No thanks are necessary."

The younger woman bent down and kissed Dewla's pretty cheek. "I shall sing all the rest of the evening," she declared, "in the hope of giving just a little word of comfort to someone else."

"And I shall watch by the window," added the white-haired lady. "Perhaps, I shall see another pair of wistful brown eyes looking in."

With this, Dewla left, her newfound friends watching her down the gaslighted street until she was out of sight.

"Mother, isn't she perfectly lovely? I never saw so sweet a face before. I wonder who she is, and why she is going away like that, with no one to see her off, and evidently no luggage, but that little, tiny bag?"

"It seems strange," returned the other, musingly. "I should, I confess, like to know the girl's story. But she has done nothing wrong – of that I am sure. Was it not well – indeed, providential, I call it – that she came in? I could not bear to think of her wandering about alone, in the city, tonight, uncertain where she might be led. She does not look like one calculated to rough it."

"Did you notice that her dress was black? I think she is in mourning, perhaps for the parents, of whom she spoke so tenderly."

"Well, dear, we can be sure of Miss Jellicoe giving her a warm welcome at the institute tonight. That should comfort the poor girl a bit. See, Martha, dear, what good your voice has done."

The younger woman came over and kissed her mother's forehead; it had such an indescribable look of serenity and peace stamped upon it, despite the many lines which time and care had written there with no ungentle hand.

"I thought her voice sounded so pretty, with the softness of the Irish accent lingering in it. I wonder what part she belongs to?" She resumed her seat at the piano, and began to sing once more, striking the chords with a firm, practiced hand.

CHAPTER II

"MRS. JONATHAN," Bella Sedley began as the great lady tried to pour words of gratitude and welcome upon her, "I have come to tell you how awfully sorry I am, but mother has developed a nasty influenza cold, and I dare not leave her just at present. That is one of the drawbacks, you see, of being an only daughter. I can't tell you how sorry we both are to have to disappoint you like this, at the eleventh hour. I waited till the doctor came, so that I might know exactly."

Mrs. Jonathan looked utterly crushed. This would disarrange her plans a little; still, plainly, Bella was not to blame.

"Never mind, my dear," she returned, "it can't be helped, I suppose. Hugh has been looking forward to seeing you in a day or two, when he is convalescent and able to enjoy a chat."

"When mother can conveniently spare me, I hope to come – that is, if the girls are still away, and you need a companion."

"In any case, my dear, you are always welcome at Trafalgar House," Mrs. Jonathan said grandly. "There was a time when I so looked forward to seeing you—" Here she stopped, as though hardly knowing how to express her sentiments.

Bella turned away, with heightened color. She thought it decidedly bad taste of her hostess to be continually throwing out suggestions of this kind.

"How cold the weather continues to remain," Bella began hastily, changing the subject. "I wonder when we shall really get some sunshine again? The calendar declares it to be springtime, but it is cold enough for Christmas. I hope our brave Queen will have a good passage across; we all feel quite proud of her."

Mrs. Jonathan shrugged her shoulders. "I have no notion that way," she declared. "I have quite sufficient talk of Paddy's-land with Dewla in the house."

"Why, Mrs. Jonathan, believe me, it is most unfashionable to talk like that nowadays. Ireland is exalted beyond measure – the land of all others, which the Queen 'delights to honor.' The up-to-date advice is 'Be Irish, or as Irish as you can.'"

The great lady frowned. "Pray, my dear, don't talk like that before Dewla or Hugh. They are both bad enough already, and this would most assuredly make them worse."

Bella smiled. "You need not be afraid. I shan't display my true feelings if you wish. But now I must go. Mother will be anxious till she gets me home again. She is always so nervous and fidgety when ill."

Mrs. Jonathan rose, too. "I am more than sorry, my dear, that we are not to have the pleasure of your society. Hugh is so much better, so we are dismissing one of the nurses today. Two nurses were not needed, especially since Dewla persists in spending all her time in the sickroom. Why, I don't know."

"She is very attentive, certainly, as a good wife should be," returned Bella, slowly.

Mrs. Jonathan puffed up dangerously. "There you go with that unpleasant talk again! Really, Bella, I believe the girl would be considered your rival – if she hadn't snatched up my son without his consent," she snarled.

Bella paused for a moment, placing her hand in Mrs. Jonathan's. "Is it not possible," she went on, "that, perhaps, you all wrong her? You see, Irish character is somewhat different than ours. They are so quick to feel either a kindness or an insult. We English are slower, and less impulsive."

The great lady drew herself up haughtily, and her florid face took a deeper hue. "You can be no judge of Dewla's disposition," she retorted hotly. "You seldom see her, and more rarely have you conversed with her. How can you possibly know?"

"Simply for two reasons," returned the girl, firmly, meeting the displeasure of Mrs. Jonathan's eyes without a waver. "First of all, I know your son would never, under any circumstance, unite himself with any but a truly good and noble woman. Secondly, the way your daughter-in-law deports herself is a recommendation in itself, for, surely, kindness is the reflex of a beautiful mind, and she is very kind."

"Oh, pooh! Speak of what you know."

"I have known and loved Hugh since the days when we played as children together. Believe me, Mrs. Jonathan, I am certain that he most truly loves his wife. I have told Etta so, more than once lately. Whenever I mention Dewla's name to him, his face changes so, and I see a look in his eyes, so tender and sweet – a look that was never there before he met her."

Bella Sedley paused. And, to be sure, that look had never been in his eyes when he'd looked at her. It had cost Bella much – so much – to speak thus, but she had braved the storm of the old lady's anger simply for Hugh's sake. It was because of her old love for him that she wanted his life to be happier than it was at present.

Mrs. Jonathan bristled all over, and it was in a very icy voice that she bade Bella farewell. She had never experienced the strength of the girl's convictions before, and the discovery was anything but pleasant to her now.

"I am most certainly glad now Bella isn't coming to stay," was the uppermost thought in the great lady's mind, as she watched the carriage roll away, the bright lights of the lamps gleaming in the gathering gloom.

With a sigh of relief, Bella Sedley sank back in her luxurious coach. "I am afraid I've 'done' for myself with the great lady," she said. "But I couldn't help it, not even if she never speaks to me again. I want Hugh to be happy, and I know it is that mother of his who is separating him from his wife. I hardly know why she is acting this way – except, perhaps, it is because he didn't marry a girl of her own choosing.

"Poor Dewla! I pity her, from my heart. At first, I thought I should hate her, because – ah! well, it doesn't matter why; but my prejudice and dislike could not hold out against the beauty of her countenance, and the winning sweetness of her frank, unfettered manner. What a time she must have, with Mrs. Jonathan for an enemy, living under the same roof, too, and needling her continually.

"Well, I daresay my intimacy with the Smith family is over now. But I don't care so much, if only Mrs. Jonathan will remember what I said, and judge her son's wife less harshly. That would bring happiness, I am sure, to poor Hugh."

Bella sighed. "What a tyrant the great lady can be! I can quite believe, now, all the current reports about her iron rule, and how all her household must bow down before her. Mrs. Wardell affirms that she kept a shop, in her young days, before she became the great Mrs. Jonathan Smith, and I daresay it is true. I perceived today an innate vulgarity that I had hardly noticed before in her superfluous nature.

"Well, I wonder how it will end – the sequel to this hastily-arranged Kerry marriage? If I did not truly believe that Hugh loves his wife with all the fervor of his strong being, I should not have placed myself in such an awkward position, calling down upon my poor head the terribleness of Mrs. Jonathan's wrath.

"But, even now, I am more than willing to risk greater dangers, for the sake of my old affection for Hugh. Ah! Hugh, you never loved me, never! I see now the foolishness of my fondly-cherished dreams. But perhaps I can still do him some good, out of … well," she added, "let us say it's out of the goodness of my heart."

CHAPTER III

At last the day seemed long,
And home seemed scarcely home,
If she did not come.
> – Christina Rossetti.

Love hangs like light about your name
    As music round the shell:
No heart can take of you a tame
    Farewell.
> -- Algernon Charles Swinburne.

"MOTHER, have you seen Dewla? She has not been here for some time." Hugh Smith looked up anxiously into Mrs. Jonathan's face.

The great lady shook her head – rather impatiently, for Bella Sedley's visit had not improved her temper. "I daresay she is moping in her own room," she retorted, "reading over that precious epistle which absorbed so much of her attention this morning."

Hugh winced as if his mother had touched a sensitive wound with careless fingers. He did not speak again for some minutes, though Mrs. Jonathan occasionally made a few remarks.

"I am afraid Bella Sedley did not care for the prospect of a sojourn here," she observed presently, with a little bitterness.

Hugh looked at her in some surprise. "Had something happened? You and she were always great friends," he said, wonderingly.

"Oh! That was before your *marriage*," she answered with a short laugh. "You see, the arrival of one Mrs. Hugh on the scene apparently changed everything."

The young man frowned. "I think you mistake, mother," he protested, quickly. "Bella and I were nothing more to each other than old friends – playmates in the days gone by. Besides, she is not the kind of girl to change in that way. I have, and always had, a very high opinion of her."

His mother flapped a dismissive hand at him. "My dear boy, men are as blind as bats. Bella just worshipped you. Ask any of your sisters. We all of us thought that it would certainly be a match."

Hugh turned away impatiently. The very suggestion annoyed him. Dewla – his little Dewie – was everything in the world to him. He could think of no other woman in her place.

Little guessing his thoughts, Mrs. Jonathan continued, "I wish the choice had fallen on her, and not that little—"

"Mother!" cried Hugh, sternly, fighting to sit up. "I cannot listen to a word breathed against my wife, even from you. What has she done to incur your bitter hostility?"

The great lady fairly quailed before the heat of his displeasure; he had seldom, if ever, spoken to her in such tones before. With a sudden jerk, she rose from her chair, and, gathering up her train; sailed from the room in high dudgeon.

Hugh, left to himself once more, shook his head and fell to wondering why Dewla did not come.

The moments slipped wearily by; he had never felt an evening so dismally long. In vain, he strained his ears, trying to catch the first sound of her soft footfall. Could she be ill? Had his mother in any way annoyed her? Such fears as these began to crowd upon his anxious brain.

Stretching out his hand, he touched the bell. Presently, a kind-faced nurse appeared. "Will you tell Mrs. Hugh that I should like to see her, if she is not very busy?"

In a few minutes, the nurse returned. "Sir, Mrs. Hugh is not to be found."

"What?" Hugh cried.

"Her room is empty," the nurse said, "and no one seems to know where she could be."

A worried look overspread the young man's face. This was strange; indeed, he was beginning to feel most uneasy. It was not like Dewla to absent herself in this manner.

"Ask Mrs. Jonathan if she would please come to me," he said. "Perhaps she may know."

The great lady came bustling in, quite excited over her daughter-in-law's disappearance, but much to Hugh's disappointment, could throw no light whatever

28

upon the subject. "I haven't seen the girl for quite a long while," she declared, vehemently, "not since I left her here with you, when Bella's carriage drew up, and I went to meet her."

An idea struck Hugh. "Perhaps she may have gone to see Mrs. Wardell."

Mrs. Jonathan rather doubted this, as Dewla never left the house without informing her, and it was too late at night for her to pay a call, especially alone, and on foot. "Not that a little trouble like that would stop a girl like her," his mother added, grumbling. However, a messenger was at once dispatched to make inquiries.

On his return, with the answer that his young mistress had not been there, Hugh became thoroughly alarmed. "Where could Dewla have gone?" he asked, his voice trembling.

Mrs. Jonathan was more uneasy than she cared to admit. She went to search in Dewla's room, and snoop through it, in hopes that she could find some indication of poor behavior on Dewla's part. Now, for the first time, her eye fell upon the little note addressed to Hugh lying upon the dressing-table.

She seized it and turned it over in her hands. Wondering very much what the contents might be, she retraced her steps towards her son's room, holding it up to every gas lamp she passed in an attempt to read the letter inside.

"Here!" Mrs. Jonathan cried, holding out the letter for him to see. "I found it on Dewla's table."

Eagerly, Hugh caught at the note. Tearing the envelope open, he read the simple words of his wife's farewell letter twice, unable, for a moment, to grasp her meaning. Then, as the truth dawned upon him, he dropped the letter and buried his face in his hands.

Seeing his distress, Mrs. Jonathan at once jumped to her own conclusion. "I always said," she cried, a ring of triumph in her voice, "that Dewla cared for no one, save that soldiering cousin of hers. You believed in her – but I knew."

"Cease, mother!" interposed the young man, all the anger of his nature roused. "Never speak to me thus again of Dewla. Remember that throwing mud at the moon cannot soil its purity, or dull its beauty."

Mrs. Jonathan flounced away to nurse her wounded feelings, while Hugh turned again to the note. He recalled Dewla's tears when she had last been with him, and cursed his blindness, to not understand what they meant.

CHAPTER IV

MISS JELLICOE of the "Eliot House" received the young stranger – sent on to her by the Hanley branch – with genial welcome.

And Dewla, as she lay her tired head upon her pillow that night, thanked God once again for the way in which His loving hand had guided her, the sweet words of the sacred song ringing in her ears still.

I'm only a sparrow – a worthless bird,
But the dear Lord cares for me!

Her last thoughts that night were of Hugh. With an earnest prayer upon her lips for his happiness with Bella, she fell into a long and dreamful sleep.

She dreamt that she and her husband were back again in beautiful Claisín. It was summertime, and the woods were carpeted with fair wildflowers. Bluebells and white anemones vied with each other in shady nooks. The trailing woodbine, with its masses of red and yellow blossom, filled the air with delicious fragrance.

Hand-in-hand through the meadows they wandered, their hearts full of gladness, until they reached the borders of the old lake around which the halo of romance was cast.

Here they sat upon a broken piece of wall, gazing in silence on the fair, sun-kissed waters.

"You have never told me that legend of the castle," Hugh said, breaking a long silence, "and I have waited so long to hear it, darling."

In her dream, she gazed up into his face to be sure that she heard aright, for had not he oftentimes laughed at what he called her "silly fancy for the wildly romantic?" But as she tried to read his face, she saw no scorn written there. Instead, there beamed upon her a tenderness, new and beautiful, in his eyes.

"Do you really want to hear about the castle-maiden of olden times?" she questioned, even still doubting the truth of his words.

For answer, he drew her head upon his shoulder and kissed her lips.

"All that you love, I love now, my Dewie," he said, with a world of tenderness in his voice.

And in her dream, she doubted him no longer. Nestling her cheek on his breast, she repeated the time-worn legend, which had ever seemed so interwoven with beauty to her childish mind. And when she had finished, he stooped and kissed her again. How happy they were – he and she – together, by the silent, rippling lake.

But, with a start, Dewla awoke to find it was only a dream, after all – nothing more.

She rose early in her strange room, and looked out the window at the busy streets below. It seemed so strange to be in an unknown city, where she had no friends or even acquaintances.

The little Bible, which her mother had loved before her, was her only friend now; and more precious she found it than ever in her life before. A wave of utter loneliness swept across her heart as she thought upon the future, stretching out so sadly before her tear-dimmed eyes.

"Oh, Hugh!" she murmured with quivering lips, "I know not if I have done right, but it was all for your sake, because I loved you so, so well."

Charlie Cooke's forgotten letter lay upon the table. She took it up, reproaching herself bitterly for want of sympathy and interest on her cousin's behalf. It was dated nearly two months back, and had evidently been delayed. It ran thus:

Dear Dewie,

I have made several attempts to write to you, but you have no idea what a difficulty it is. So far, I am well, thank God, though, how I have escaped is indeed a marvel to myself. I think it is in answer to your sweet little cousin's prayers. Ah, how often I think of your farewell promise; and I know you are not one to forget your word. Dewie, I had truly no conception whatever of the awfulness of war or the piteous sight of a battlefield; but I will not sadden you with details, for I dare say you read the accounts given in the papers.

We were all terribly cut up by the death of Lord Roberts' brave son, one of the many of Erin's sons to fight and fall for Queen and country. The battle of Colenso was terrible. It was a horrible position to attack. We had a river to cross, under fire, followed by a flat slope of two miles without a vestige of cover. The enemy was attacking from the safety of a succession of steep low hills, covered with bush. Every hill was entrenched, and their whole position the shape of a horseshoe, so that our advance was into a converging fire. I don't believe any troops could have taken it. Not a Boer to be seen – that is their game. We are simply human targets for their bullets and shells.

After the battle – which was one of the bloodiest – poor Lieutenant Roberts was found badly wounded. They got him with difficulty into the Nullah, where he lay from eleven to half-past four – no water, not a breath of air, no particle of shade. The sun, I am sure, could not be hotter even in India. A knife could not be held in the bare hand in that heat. It was a terrible day, and seemed interminable. What it must have been for the badly wounded, I dare not try to think.

But enough of this, Cousin Dewie. I only beg that you would still pray for me? for you know not how we need it.

You see my letter has to be postponed. Only today has the letter containing the news of your marriage reached me. Accept my very sincerest congratulations. You see, I did not prove a false prophet after all. Something seemed to tell me that such would be the case. What a lucky dog this Smith must consider himself! I envy him his luck.

I promised you a Persian cat, did I not? Well, no chance of fulfilling my promise out here; you must wait till my return – that is, if I do! For who can say out here which of us will? But we all hope for the best.

I have just re-addressed my envelope to Mrs. Hugh Smith – how strange it looks. I suppose, when we meet again, I shall hardly recognize my merry little cousin, transformed into a stately lady of fashion, and English withal!

Well, I shan't forget the cat! I mean to bring you back all kinds of funny things – relics of the war, and some of the native curios. I have begun my collection already – on a small scale, of course!

Write and tell me more about yourself. Strange, that I should have got the paper containing the sad notice of dear Uncle's death before your own letter, and news of your marriage so late, though, I think, they were sent off almost at the same lime. But all our mails out here are so erratic, and no wonder either.

I cannot think of dear old Claisín without you both. It was the only home I ever knew. How good my kind Uncle ever was to me, a poor orphan lad. I have never met his equal. No wonder the poor country people loved him as they did. I think he was a kind of saint to their simple minds. He was a good man, if ever there breathed one. You would have felt his loss sadly, had not another come forward to fill the great gap in your desolate heart.

Dewie, you will never be half as happy as I should wish you to be, my dear cousin.

Surely, this is a curious letter, and yet it is written under the sound of distant gunfire. God bless you; think of me sometimes. Tell Hugh I hope to make his acquaintance "when the war is over." Till then, fare-thee-well.

With every kind wish,
From your affectionate Cousin,
CHARLIE.

Dewla sat with the letter in her hand. A tear dropped upon the page and blurred a word or two.

"Dear old Charlie," she thought. "Would that we could have ever remained as happy children, in the quiet shelter of our secluded Irish home among the woods of Claisín, playing in the gleefulness of our merry hearts at being grown-up. You, with sword in hand, a 'Soldier of the Queen,' and I the wife of some noble knight. Ah, we little knew how different the realization of our fondly-cherished dreams would be, bye-and-bye.

"Someday, perhaps, the dark clouds may roll away, and Hugh and I may yet be happy together. Oh, if such might be the case, surely, I could bear anything now, for Hugh is everything to me, and his love the sweetest treasure which earth can give. God bless him, now and always."

> If I can trust mine ownself with your fate,
> Shall I not rather trust it in God's hand?
> Without Whose Will one lily doth not stand,
> Nor sparrow fall at his appointed date.
> -- Christina Rossetti.

CHAPTER V

DEWLA'S great ambition now was to become a writer, so that in the future Hugh might read something which had fallen from her pen, and thus feel proud of her.

It was this hope which helped to keep her from sinking into despair, and this was the reason why she had come to Manchester, in order to have a personal interview with the editor to whom she had sent her MS. She knew little indeed of the many disappointments which usually attend the beginning of an author's career.

Her father had contributed little sketches occasionally to *The Strand*, which were eagerly picked up because of their literary merit; so, in her happy dreams of future success, she hardly counted upon any discouragement at the outset.

Under Miss Jellicoe's kind directions, she reached the editor's offices sometime about midday. It was not until she stood irresolute at the entrance that she began to feel somewhat timid of the task lying before her.

"Will he be too busy to pay attention to an unknown individual like me?" she wondered, slowly ascending the steep stairs, step by step.

In large letters, hallway up, she read the name of the editorial offices. Pausing, she touched a bell. Presently a clerk appeared.

"Can I see the editor?" she inquired, trying to keep the quaver out of her voice.

"Can I see the Editor?" she enquired.

The young man glanced at her curiously, invited her to sit down, and disappeared into an inner room.

Dewla was beginning to feel nervous, though she strove hard not to think at all of herself. It seemed quite an age before the clerk appeared again. He merely inquired her name and the nature of her visit, before vanishing once again through the imposing door, which bore the one word in gilt letters: "Private."

Dewla looked about her. What a busy place it seemed; piles of papers and books lay everywhere. It had been newly done-up, evidently, for a decided smell of fresh paint pervaded the whole premises. The room looked so bright and clean, despite the city smoke and dirt. She strove not to read the papers that lay closest to her, for she could see that they were stories sent in from other contributors – many, *many* stories – which made her nervousness start up again.

"You can step this way, please," said the fair-haired clerk as he reappeared, and he held the door open for Dewla to pass through.

A grave-faced man wearing glasses rose courteously from his chair beside a table strewn with papers, and bowed.

Dewla felt her cheeks burning. "I sent a manuscript," she began, rather tremulously, "hoping it might be suitable for your magazine."

"Sunshine and Shadow," he returned kindly, his shrewd eyes detecting the painful shyness of her manner.

His friendly tone set Dewla more at ease as she took a seat.

"You are Irish, Mrs. Smith?" he said. "I can tell that at once. Do you usually write about your own country, and its people?"

"I have never tried before," she faltered. "This was my first effort."

"Indeed?" He seemed surprised, she thought. "Just at present," he went on, "Irish tales are acceptable. Indeed, there is a decided demand for any stories about the Emerald Isle. I should advise you to continue to write as you began. An Irish heroine, as well as Irish soldiers, are quite up-to-date."

"Oh, I am glad to hear it," she said softly.

"At any rate, I have looked through your tale, and have decided to accept it."

Dewla breathed more freely. She looked up with a gleam of sunshine in her wistful eyes. "You have?"

"Indeed! How soon can you let me have another? This time, let the subject be thoroughly Irish."

"I can begin at once," she cried in low, glad tones. "Oh, I am so glad, for I do so want to be a writer."

He smiled, very much interested in his contributor. "Hanley is where you live, is it not?" he inquired, glancing at a letter lying open upon his desk.

Dewla started. "Not now," she stammered eagerly, "for I am staying in Manchester – for a while, at least."

"Indeed?" he returned, and then wrote down her present address. "Let me have your manuscript as soon as possible," he said, as Dewla rose to depart.

With glad, quick steps, the girl descended the long stairs. Her first interview with an editor hadn't been such a terrible experience, after all. Now her future did not seem so very dark. Perhaps, some day, Hugh might yet be proud of her, and thus his love might be won back once more. Ah, was this not the great, earnest prayer of her loving, warm heart?

Once she was home, Dewla bent over her sheets of foolscap with a very thoughtful look in her bonny eyes. "The editor asked for something Irish! What shall it be?" It seemed so difficult to choose a subject.

Suddenly the memory of her dream came back. She at once decided upon the legend of the castle buried in the rippling waters of the old lough at Claisín.

THE LEGEND OF THE LOUGH

In olden times, there stood, nigh to the village of Claisín, a quaint old castle that was fast falling into decay and ruin. Among its ivy-grown turrets, rooks built their nests. White owls emerged at dusk to break the stillness of the night with their weird and dismal cries.

In this castle dwelt an impoverished knight with his daughter, Sheila. Poor and proud was he – embittered, too, by his gradual losses of land and wealth. His last and only hope now was, that Sheila, more beautiful than all the maidens round about, should wed a wealthy suitor, retrieving their fallen fortunes and replenishing the empty coffers of their ancient house.

But all these lofty ambitions and fondly-cherished dreams were rudely dispelled, when Brian Esmond, a distant kinsman of his own, and poorer than the knight, demanded the fair Sheila's hand in marriage.

Displeased as he was at the prospect of such a union, he also foresaw that opposition would be fruitless, for already the young man had confessed his love in secret, and Sheila had returned his devotion with all the strength of her loyal heart.

Thus was the old knight forced to consent to their betrothal, but only on condition that the marriage should not take place for the space of a full year. Meanwhile, Brian – a soldier, strong and brave – must go and fight his country's battles, for these were turbulent times in Ireland.

One fair September morn, the lovers parted beneath the great spreading lilac boughs, green with mossy age, and lichen-grown. Their hearts were filled with mingled feeling of pain and hope – pain for the present moment, with its sorrowful farewells, and hope for the untried, rosy future.

And thus they parted. He went forth to win his spurs, athirst for glory and honor, and fired by the sweetness of her trusting love; while Sheila tarried at home, spinning amongst her maids. Whilst her fingers would glide in work, she would weave, by fancy's wondrous power, such fair and lovely dreams as find existence alone in a maiden's heart.

As the days went by, there came no tidings of the absent Brian. All in vain, Sheila would sit beside her latticed window panes, with listless hands folded upon her unfinished work, watching sadly with strained eyes, for his return.

But he never, never came. Nor did he send one word, one message!

In secret now she wept and prayed, her wools and distaff lying unheeded at her feet. No longer could either hands or brain weave pictures fair and sweet.

In her father's presence alone, her grief was ever stayed, for bravely she strove to hide from his stern eyes her wan cheeks now grown pale with weary waiting. Ah! Well she knew that he had no sympathy for all her misery.

Thus the weary months dragged by, bringing with them no tidings, no change in the monotony of her sorrow. Her smileless face grew more spirit-like, and her dark eyes were darker still with midnight shadows.

At length, there came a day when her father called her to him.

"Sheila." He spake roughly without a glance upon her troubled brow. "A year has waned since thy faithless lover left thee."

She turned her head away and shivered. There was no need to remind her of how long Brian had been gone. Had she not counted each weary week, not by days or hours only?

"I told thee he was dead," continued the knight, looking with relentless eyes upon the girl's drooping head. "Thou didst not hearken to me then. Dost thou believe now?"

Sheila's slight frame quivered as though with pain, but she made no reply. Her lips were pressed together tightly, sealed by anguish.

Her father moved uneasily in his chair, for his daughter's silence provoked him not a little.

"My Lord of Muskerry seeks to wed with thee. Thou must listen to his suit, for he is rich beyond compare, and most noble withal."

At these words, she shrank back, as though he had dealt her a deadly blow, leaning against the darkly paneled wall, her eyes full of fear, and tear dimmed.

"Thou must cease to pine for your worthless Brian," he went on, hurriedly. "Give my Lord of Muskerry a kindly hearing; he is more worthy of thy love than young Esmond, who hath sent to thee no token, no message, this twelve-month past."

At this, Sheila's eyes flashed, and she raised her head proudly, but, meeting the coldness of his gaze, her courage failed; she knew her father's nature too well, and read her fate in the stern lines of his face.

"Thou must forget thy lover, Brian," he cried, his brow darkening. "Dost harken to me, Sheila?"

She spake. "Give me yet a little time," she pleaded, wildly, her eyes heavy with unshed tears. "Perchance that, even yet, he may return."

But the knight, already dazzled with visions of the riches of the wealthier suitor, was not to be won by her entreaties.

"Thou hast already had four seasons wherein to wait," he returned harshly, "and they have but made thee wan and thin; wherefore should I prolong thy useless vigils? Yet, as thou askest, I will grant to thee still another season. But remember, daughter, when Yuletide draweth nigh, thou must become the bride of the noble Lord of Muskerry."

Then Sheila stole blindly from the room, her face most white, looking like one who had received a death warrant.

Her love for him no words could break.
Her trust in him no doubts could shake.
More fair was he than all beside.
Most dear to her, his promised bride.

Now autumn has faded into winter; the months of waiting have come and gone without one word from Brian. The snows of a dying year lie thick upon the hilltops.

No longer durst the timid maiden hold out against her parent's wishes, whose slightest command had ever been her law. In truth, she hath no strength to resist longer, though her heart is nigh to breaking with its weight of grief, for on the coming morrow must she wed my Lord of Muskerry.

The night was wild and stormy, but, ever and anon, the silvery moon shone out from behind dark clouds with clear and brightening rays.

Beside her latticed window wept the lonely maid; her upturned face was almost as white as the gleaming snows on yonder peats. Her small hands were clasped together, and now and again a moan of pain escaped her lips.

The chamber was laden with the perfumes of delicate flowers sent by her suitor to adorn her wedding gown; their odors of heavy sweetness seemed almost to suffocate her.

A strange longing for a breath of pure air took possession of her restless spirit. Slipping with noiseless tread along the deserted passages, she gained, at length, a side door that opened out upon the neglected garden.

The icy blast of the winter's storm swept about her slight form with relentless force, but she, almost unconscious of its thrilling touch, went forth, thinking only of those happy summer hours when she and Brian had wandered beneath those same old spreading trees, their hearts so full of gladness.

The world had seemed all bright with sunshine then, and gay with many a flower; but now, the winter's sky was overcast. All blossoms were gone. All that remained were the bitterness of withered leaves and shriveled buds of hope, long dead. Each spot of this deserted garden was sacred in her eyes, because of memories sweet. How oft had their childish feet trodden together this moss-strewn pathway!

There were the holly trees – now red with clustering berries – beneath whose shade they had lingered to bid a last farewell. And here, too, under the leafless lilacs was the old magic well, about which such strange traditions were ever whispered. It was at this crystal spring that Brian and she had pledged their troth.

Flinging herself upon the damp, cold earth, she knelt upon the very spot where first he had breathed those tender words of love to her.

"Oh, Brian, Brian!" she wailed, wringing her hands in an agony of despair. "I am true to you still; too true in heart and love." And the moaning wind, as it swept along, seemed to bear and carry her cry of pain, and echo it afar.

Mute tears rolled down her cheeks, unchecked at first. But when she raised her hand to wipe them away, there slipped from her finger a ring – the ring which Brian had given to her – for she had grown thin, and it was looser now than when his hand had placed it there. Into the shallow waters it splashed and sank.

With affrighted haste, she hung over the clear well, but could see naught of her lost treasure. All in vain, she peered about, guided only by the fitful moonbeams; the ring was not to be seen.

Oh, Brian, Brian, *I am true to you, still!*

At the well's mouth there lay a stone, and thinking perchance it had rolled beneath, she tried to move it. At first, it resisted all her force and efforts, but, as she struggled, it yielded. There, half-hidden in the muddy bed, she espied with joy the gleam of her diamond ring, flashing in the pale light.

With a little cry, she rescued it, caressing passionately the cold, wet jewel, dearer to her heart than aught else, because of him who gave it.

In her excitement, she neglected to restore again the stone to its former place. Rising hastily to her feet, she endeavored to retrace her steps through the thickly tangled grasses and weeds towards the castle.

A wonderful sense of rest seemed all at once to brood upon her troubled breast. No longer did the dread of the morrow haunt her mind; she seemed almost to have forgotten its existence, and its terror. With childish pleasure she gazed up at the lowering sky, against which the old trees tossed their leafless branches, swaying to and fro, in the fury of the gale. It was a weird and ghostly night, but Sheila felt no alarm. With a lighter heart than she had known for many a day, she bounded on.

How still was the old castle. One by one, the red lights faded from its windows, until now it lay wrapped in somber darkness, and the whole household slept. Only Sheila was astir.

With noiseless steps, she mounted the winding stairs, not pausing till she had gained her own chamber. Here, by the rush-light's flame, she gazed afresh upon the ring, a smile so sweet upon her parted lips.

"Oh, Brian," she whispered, "'twere surely given back to me, in token that naught shall ever sever us now. I am thine, thine only, till death – sweet death – shall bear me to thee."

Then she wept a little, but now her tears were those of joy most pure.

How the storm raged outdoors, ever increasing in its fury. Even in her slumbers. Sheila seemed to hear the shrieking of the wind, as it swept around the old castle, shaking with ruthless grasp the time-worn casements. But mingled now with the furious gale came the noise of rushing waters. The very foundations of the ancient edifice quivered and shook like a leaf.

But Sheila only smiled more sweetly in her dreamless sleep, and pressed her Brian's ring closer to her breast. Storm and grief seemed powerless now to hurt or harm her more.

The day dawned, but no bridal morn awoke for Sheila.

When the winter's sun arose, it shone down with cold light upon a strange scene of desolation. It appeared as though the very floodgates of the swollen river had been all unlocked during the hours of darkness. The castle, inmates, and garden alike, had been swallowed up, for no trace remained of them. A wide expanse of deep, troubled waters covered the place where so lately stood the old walls.

People flocked from afar to gaze, affrighted, on so terrible a spectacle. With bated breath, they whispered together in little groups, conjecturing vaguely what it all meant. Had the storm upheaved the well? Had the river, so swollen with recent rains, burst its bounds? All in vain, they wondered – but none could tell, nor solve the dark mystery.

With bated breath they whispered together.

But hark ye to my legend's closing line:
'Twas said, by some, in olden times,
That after dusk at each Yuletide
The spirits fair of Brian and his Bride
Were seen to wander, clothed in white,
Beside those moonlit waters bright,
And at the dawn of breaking day
Hand in hand they fled away.
While some, I learn, did most affirm

That they could oft and oft discern
The crumbling turrets, dark and grey
Which far beneath those waters lay.

CHAPTER VI

Oh, pleasant have the hours of my early childhood been,

When all around me seem'd enrobed in brightly-glittering sheen.

When a thousand rainbow tints were in every simple flower,

And a thousand new delights came with every sunny hour;

When I thought the merry birds trilled their carols all for me,

And with heart and voice I joined in their joyous melody.

-- Frances R. Havergal

LONG after Dewla had written the last word of her manuscript, she sat with her head bowed upon her folded arms. Recalling this old, favorite story of her childhood brought back her great love for her beautiful country home. How intensely she longed for even one glimpse of the shining, rippling lake.

Soon – in a few short weeks – the trees would be bursting into leaf, and all nature would awaken beneath the warm caresses of the bright sun rays. Oh, that she might be there, to see, once again, the dear old orchard, clothed afresh with tender blossoms.

"But there is nothing keeping me from my home," Dewla murmured, raising her head in new excitement.

Surely, she must go! She could never remain here, in the bustle and smoke of the great city. The ceaseless noise of the never-ending traffic disturbed her spirit.

Yes! She was quickly making up her mind to return once more to the peaceful shelter of the dear Kerry hills. How glad old Hannah would be to see her – and all the others, too. Would they think it strange – her coming home again, and alone? But no; they were not the kind of people to ask questions, and no one need know the truth. She would be "Dewla" to them still, and that was all the simple folk needed.

It was with far more courage than before that Dewla sought and entered the editor's office the second time. The fair-haired clerk recognized her; he even smiled in return to her gentle words of greeting.

The editor was engaged, so she had some time to wait.

Looking through the high window, she contemplated the crowded street below. Hugh had spoken of taking her to London; but surely this was a city busy enough to satisfy anyone. Streams of cabs and wagons followed each other in quick succession – there came no pause in the rapid progress. How different to the quiet of Claisín, with its green meadows where the gentle cattle grazed undisturbed.

Looking down upon the busy city, Dewla realized how oddly comfortable she felt, in these strange offices, in this strange city. She felt nervous, certainly, but as she looked down at the close-written pages she held in her hands, she also felt pride.

The sneering face of Hugh's mother rose up in her mind. She could hear all the cutting things she would say if she could see Dewla here.

"No," Dewla said quietly, looking around the quiet office, strewn with manuscripts and books. A glow of pride warmed her heart. This was her world. This was where she belonged. Soon she would be home again, writing stories as she sat in her uncle's chair. She would walk again under the boughs of the friendly old trees, untroubled by the ghost of Mrs. Jonathan.

At length the editor received Dewla kindly; he was already somewhat interested in his new contributor.

"Are you remaining long in Manchester, Mrs. Smith?" he inquired, glancing up from the manuscript that she had brought him for inspection.

Dewla shook her head. Then, after a moment's hesitation, she said, "I made up my mind, yesterday, to return to Kerry. I like it so much better than the noisy life of a city."

"But there are lovely country parts in England, as well as Ireland," he returned, with an amused smile. "You should visit Devonshire, for instance. Cloveley is one of the most delightful places possible. You would simply revel in the beauties of Hartland Abbey and its surrounding country."

Dewla looked slightly skeptical. "Perhaps. But so far, I have seen nothing since I came to England that is worthy to be compared with my Irish home," she answered in rather a decided tone of voice.

"Well, then, if you really are returning, would it not be a good plan to try and arrange your departure so that you might manage to witness something of the Royal visit of our Queen to Dublin? It might be useful. You could write about it, you know, in the future."

But Dewla winced, for had not Hugh talked of their going across together? And now she was here alone. The thought struck her sadly, and her lips trembled.

"I have just been reading,"' continued the editor, "an extract from an old paper, which gives Her Majesty's own account of her visit to Queenstown in August 1849. She remarks that Cork, fifty years ago, was not at all like an English town but looked rather foreign. In her concluding paragraph, she refers to the character of the crowds, and pays a high tribute to the beauty of the women of this city – 'the crowd is a noisy, excitable, but very good-humored one, running and pushing about, and laughing, talking, and shrieking. The beauty of the women is very remarkable indeed, and struck us at once – such beautiful dark eyes and hair, and such fine teeth. They wear no bonnets, and generally long blue cloaks.'"

The editor paused, and then, adjusting his glasses, said: "If you are in Dublin for the Royal visit, I shall be very pleased to accept, from you, your own impression of the reception given to our Gracious Sovereign. You could weave it into a story, I think."

Dewla looked interested. "Yes," she answered slowly. "I think I could, perhaps."

"I congratulate you on the rising popularity of your nation," he said. "The tide has surely turned at last, in favor of Paddy's Land!"

"The bravery of our soldiers has done that," she replied, thinking, for the moment, of her cousin Charlie. "And now, England, in the very person of its Sovereign, holds out the hand of friendship to the sister isle. I know my people well enough to anticipate a warm and enthusiastic welcome."

"Indeed? Then you are more sanguine than we are. For my part, I rather tremble for the safety of our Queen."

Dewla's dark eyes flashed a little, and she tilted her nose scornfully. "The chivalrous behavior of Irishmen towards women is well known, and has been the undying theme through all ages, of both poet and bard. Surely, Moore was right when he sang:

"And blest forever is she who relied
Upon Erin's honor and Erin's pride."

The editor laughed. "You are most patriotic, certainly. Well, a few days more will decide everything, and all the world will be watching anxiously the attitude of Ireland towards her time-honored Sovereign. Somehow, you inspire me with confidence. But to return to the subject in question: When do you purpose starting for Kingstown?"

"You mean Dún Laoghaire," she murmured under her breath.

"What's that?" the editor asked, smiling.

"I mean to say, I will go as soon as possible, in consideration of your request. And I hope I shall be able to give you all you ask."

"Oh, doubtless; but don't be too partial, and don't mention the big display of blackthorn sticks, which are sure to be flourished in the air by alien spirits. You call them 'shillelaghs,' don't you?"

"I am afraid you'll have to visit Ireland yourself, in order to acquire a correct pronunciation of the word," returned Dewla, archly. "As a matter of face, perhaps I shall, now that our *brave* Queen is setting us such a good example. I shouldn't be surprised, indeed, if Ireland becomes the happy hunting-field for tourists this season."

He laughed again. "You sign your own name," he continued, glancing at the papers she had brought. "That is better, I think, than choosing a nom-de-plume. 'Dewla' is a rather uncommon name. Is it Irish?"

Dewla bowed, and then rose to leave.

"You are rather fortunate in writing Irish tales at present. A year ago, there would have been little or no demand for them; but just now, why, you can't send me too many. War stories are becoming a bit too general, as the public wants something new always. Ireland is the very latest."

"Poor old Ireland!" thought she, as she wended her way through the crowded thoroughfare. "May this gracious and kindly-planned visit of our beloved Sovereign lift forever the dark cloud that has hung so long over thy beautiful land!"

CHAPTER VII

Talk what you please of future spring,
And sun-warmed sweet to-morrow—
Stripp'd bare of hope and everything,
No more to laugh, no more to sing,
I sit alone with sorrow.
                    —Christina Rossetti

I know not how to tell thee!
Shame rises in my face, and interrupts
The story of my tongue.
                    – Thomas Otway

NOW that Dewla had mysteriously vanished, the whole of Trafalgar household was in a state of suspense. Hugh was driven to distraction. Where could his wife be? This remained a problem which none could solve.

He wired immediately to Claisín, but the returning message said that Dewla had not returned to the old home; nor did she do so, as the days dragged slowly by. Where else could she be? She had no friends in England – of that he was positive.

Mrs. Jonathan summoned her daughters back at once. She greatly feared this trouble would bring on a relapse. Hugh was far from well yet, though he insisted on leaving his room and coming downstairs, contrary to the doctor's orders. In vain, he tortured himself night and day, imagining reason after reason as the reason for the suddenness of her flight.

Now that he had lost his winsome little wife – only now did he fully realize how precious she had become to his heart. How he missed the music of her voice, with its soft Irish accent, and the sound of her step, always quick and light!

One day, Bella Sedley called. Finding him in the study alone, brooding over his loss, she resolved to broach the forbidden subject of Dewla's mysterious departure – for reasons of her own, which she dared not mention in Mrs. Jonathan's presence.

Hugh listened to her preliminary words of sympathy, wondering rather that she had ventured on a question of the kind. Perhaps, she divined his thoughts, for she said, abruptly, "I have felt very guilty, ever since the moment I first heard of Dewla's disappearance. I have longed to tell you something which, perhaps, may throw some light upon it all."

Hugh looked up eagerly. What could she mean?

Then Bella related the conversation which passed between herself and his mother; how she had felt positive Dewla must have overheard, because of her sharp cry, as though wrung from one in pain, and her rapid flight of steps along the hall, when his mother had declared that Hugh did not love Dewla, but loved only Bella. And then Mrs. Jonathan herself had insisted that Bella come to visit, only adding insult to injury.

Hugh's face grew paler as he listened. Here, as last, was a clue to the whole thing; for well he knew Dewla's sweet, sensitive nature, and how it would gall her proud spirit to imagine his mother spoke the truth, and that he loved her no longer.

And he, Hugh, had not even realized Dewla's distress at this news. Now that Bella had revealed all, now he saw the ways in which he, himself, had seemed to give truth to his mother's words – how he himself had told Dewla how happy he would be to see the woman who was clearly her rival!

Covering his face with his hands, he groaned aloud. Now he understood the purport of her tear-stained, hurried note. She had gone, poor, simple child, in order to set him free.

Long after Bella had departed, he sat, lost in thought, trying to devise some plan of action. She must be traced and found – but how? It was strange, he mused, that she had not returned to Kerry, the one place of all the earth, that she loved best.

And as he sat there, back to his mind came the vision of a white-robed girl who had come forth from the gloomy portals of the antiquated hall to receive him with outstretched hand, bidding him welcome in shy, sweet tones.

He it was who had torn her from the happy, sheltered home of her forefathers, and brought her here – to what?

He shuddered, as he thought now upon the daily tortures which she had been called upon to endure since her advent to Trafalgar House; petty trials, perhaps, to another, but far more than that to one of Dewla's singular purity of mind and innate refinement. And he had sat by and allowed the taunts to continue.

Why had he brought her here? Ah! That was where the great mistake lay – the beginning of all their misery. Poor little Dewla! No wonder she grew sad and silent, and the roses died upon her cheeks.

Well he could recollect her fervently-expressed hope ere they reached their destination, on that wintry night when he brought her home, that "his mother might love her!" He had laughed within himself at the very folly of such a doubt upon her part, for, surely, to know Dewla was to love her also!

So he had thought then.

Alas! He had not understood his mother's nature, nor had he thought of her secret reason why she so hated the whole Irish nation. In her girlhood, she had loved an Irish lad who had not returned her affections, but treated her with cold indifference. Therefore, her love soon turned to hatred, and not for him alone, but also extended to all his race!

She had only wanted a mother's love, but instead Hugh had watched as his mother had inflicted a thousand little cruelties upon her. And, to make matters even worse, he had believed his mother when she said that Dewla loved her cousin more. He had never bothered to ask Dewla the truth – instead had chosen to treat her with coldness and indifference.

Slowly, as the young man pondered thus – thinking on the past, hoping for the future – the remembrance of Dewla's prayerful spirit, as well as her faith and trustfulness in God's love and power, flashed upon him.

How often he had found her in her room, quietly praying.

Bowing his head reverently, he, too, became a supplicant at the throne of grace, praying to shed his old, mistrustful ways, and praying to find her in hopes that he could earn her forgiveness.

CHAPTER VIII

LORD TENNYSON ON THE QUEEN.
Revered, beloved – O you that hold
A nobler office upon earth
Than arms, or power of brains or birth
Could give the warrior kings of old...

May children of our children say
She wrought her people lasting good.

Her court was pure, her life serene,
God gave her peace; her land reposed;
A thousand claims to reverence closed
In her as Mother, Wife, and Queen!

DEWLA SMITH had never, in her wildest dreams, imagined anything like what the reception really would be that awaited Queen Victoria, when she set foot once again on Irish soil. Its magnificence, enthusiasm, and real true heartiness baffled all description.

She stood crowded among her countrymen behind two rows of guards bristling with swords, the very air around her filled with the exuberant waving of handkerchiefs and derby hats. Little children were raised up to sit upon their fathers' shoulders, in the cool spring day.

In wonderment, she stood amid the gigantic crowds and listened to the endless roar of warm applause. The whole air was filled with ringing bursts of cheers as the spirited, high-stepping horses came trotting in with their guards sitting straight and tall on their backs, and the white feathers that adorned their helmets blowing in the spring breeze.

Oh! How glad she was. Tears of joy filled her eyes, because, in spite of all that people had said, Ireland, dear Ireland, was true, not only to its great and noble Sovereign, but also to itself, and its own honor. Not one note of discord marred the moment of triumph and rejoicing.

Then the cheering and handkerchief waving swelled as a new carriage came into view on the street. "The Queen! The Queen!" they shouted.

Dewla, from her distant standpoint, could just catch a glimpse of the kind, motherly face of our beloved Queen, looking tired and pale, but, nevertheless, bowing and smiling, in answer to the rolling volleys of cheers which greeted her on all sides. The sun was shining down upon the gay scene, with almost summer-like ardor, and she sat under the shade of a little umbrella.

Dewla had never heard such bursts of cheering. Surely, she thought, when the English people see and hear of this, they will believe that Ireland is loyal and true to the very core. This was, indeed, a real test.

"How will Ireland greet the Queen?" had been the burning question of the day. How? Not with a mere roar of noise, but with such a united heart, that its emotion half-choked its voice. There were tears in the cheer, because the great concourse of people knew and understood the sympathy which had touched and prompted the kind heart of their Sovereign Queen, to come among them; sympathy, because so many of Erin's brave soldiers had fought, and died, on South Africa's distant shore, in serving under England's flag.

It was this sympathy, and her tender recognition of their brave loyalty, that won all Irish hearts. Surely, the very hardest must give way before her gentle sway. The true voice of Ireland had spoken. Politicians may say what they will, but never can that great sob of welcome die out; none who were present could ever forget it.

Queen Victoria's entrance to her Irish capital was one splendid and undiluted ride of brilliant triumph and joy. It was a red-letter day in the annals of the city. Surely, it must be the opening of a new epoch in Ireland's eventful career. No English city could have honored Her Majesty with more exceeding loyalty and devotion.

"I am afraid I can never write about it," thought Dewla in some dismay. "It all seems too beautiful and grand." And she looked about her helplessly, at the great magnificence of the costly decorations, the many flags blowing in the wind, the soldiers that stood, stock still, to separate the grand procession from the people, and the many proud horses in the parade who pricked up their ears and kept sidling sideways in their excitement.

Surely, such general evidence of rejoicing, it may be said, without exaggeration, could not possibly be exceeded in any part of Her Majesty's dominions. Ah, surely, it was a proud day for old Ireland.

Across Dewla's mind flashed the old, familiar words, from the Book of Esther: "Whom the king delighteth to honor."

And then another verse suggested itself: "The reward of humility, and the fear of the Lord, are riches and honor and life."

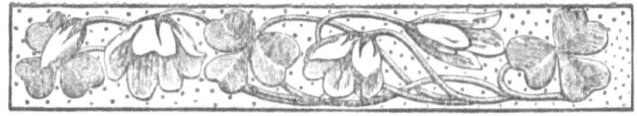

Welcome, Victoria, Queen-Empress, to Erin!
Céad míle, and céad míle fáilte to you!
Long have we waited and watched for your coming,
With love of the leal, and trust of the true.

Can't you hear the glad beat of the heart of the nation,
As it thrills at the sound of your magical name?
It will rise from ashes of sore tribulation,
To meet you and greet you with highest acclaim.

Oh, mother, queen-mother, our bleeding hearts turn to you,
For we know that your heart has been bleeding with ours;
But at the sound of your footsteps we bury our sorrow,
That your path may be bright with our sunshine and flowers!

Oh, mother, Queen-mother! God grant you the sunshine
And incense of blossoms, most fragrant and sweet;
The sunlight and bloom of a nation's devotion,
And are emblems of shamrock to spring at your feet.
                         --Theila

It was evening at Claisín. Old Hannah had just
spread her evening meal, and only waited for the kettle
to boil. It was a large, old-fashioned kitchen, such as is
seldom seen nowadays. Everything was bright and
shining, clean as the faithful old woman's hands could
make them.

What a pleasant face she had: rosy as a girl's, with
thick black hair almost untouched with grey. Her
petticoat of blue homemade flannel was short, over

which her rather faded magenta skirt was worn in true fish-wife style. Across her shoulders was pinned a small check shawl, cornerwise, while her head was adorned with a large white, frilled cap, around which a black ribbon was tied. She stood with her back towards the door, her eyes fixed dreamily upon the singing kettle in hopes that it would boil faster, because she dearly wanted that tea.

A step sounded in the passage, but she did not hear. Then a figure, slight and graceful, paused upon the threshold of the door.

"Hannah!" called out a dear, familiar voice.

The old nurse fairly jumped off her feet, wheeling round in dumb amazement. But it was only for a moment that speech forsook her.

"Sure, n' me darling, if it isn't your own self, I'm glad to see. An' how's every bit of you?" she cried, taking the girl's slim fingers within her rough palms, and gazing into the pale, beautiful face, raised to hers. "An' where's himself? – Mister Hugh, I means. Well! Well! sure enough, me dream's come true, for didn't I dream, these three nights running, that the Queen herself came here? So I did, without a word of a lie!"

"Shure, an' me darlint, if it is not your own self!"

A smile flitted across Dewla's face. To be speaking to her dear nurse again was such a pleasure, such solace to her heart.

"I am a very poor substitute, I fear," Dewla said playfully. "You surely would not compare me with our great Sovereign?"

The old peasant woman touched the girl's arm. "In the good auld times, 'twas said The O'Donough had no equal. Ah! And 'twasn't alike, either! But times is changed, and, as the Scripture says, 'the mighty is fallen.' But Miss Dewie – ma'am, I means, asking your pardon – where has you been? Sure, but himself – Mister Hugh – has been a-sending telegrams most days, asking if you'd come."

Dewla started a little. Hugh missed her then, or he would not have troubled to make inquiries.

"So says I to meself, says I, sure, an' Miss Dewie is on her way. So I up an' I does your room. 'Tis all ready, an' fit for the Queen herself."

Dewla's heart beat fast. "Show me the messages he sent, Hannah," she said in unsteady tones.

"To be sure, Miss – ma'am. They're all together on the table in yer own room. I'll bring your tea in a moment, Miss De – ma'am, I means – an' a nice griddle cake, as I made meself today."

Dewla went upstairs, looking around her in childish pleasure at her dear old home, running her hand over the smooth banister. In her own room – the very room where she had slept on that memorable night when summoned to her dying father's bedside – she found Hugh's anxious queries. Spreading them out, she read them one by one, looking at them tenderly as though his own hand had written the penciled words.

The slanting sunbeams stole in and touched her bowed head. She fain would linger thus, but Hannah's kindly voice roused her, announcing that tea was all ready in the old dining-room.

The kind-hearted woman watched her beloved mistress with anxious eyes. How changed she was! The bonny brightness had flown from her face – instead, it was wistful and sad.

"Why is this?" Hannah mused. "Could it be that she is not happy?"

Dewla spoke but little of her English home. "It was very grand," she said, "and costly." That was all she had to say about that, and she asked quickly of the news of all the old friends of her youth. This made old Hannah suspicious, and she thought all the more.

Only when Dewla told about the wonderful reception so loyally accorded to the Queen, did her face brighten.

"Oh! It was splendid!" she cried, enthusiastically. "I felt so proud! Oh, surely, nurse, brighter days will now dawn upon our land, for are we are a people 'whom the Queen delighteth to honor?' These words rang so in my mind on Wednesday, as I thought upon her kindness in undertaking such a long journey, just to show her tender sympathy and deep appreciation of what the Irish soldiers have done for her in South Africa."

The old woman nodded her head slowly. "There be them as says different in these parts; but says I, 'tis the likes of them, says I, that upset the country, first with their speechafying, making simple folks that didn't know better believe their wild talk. I don't know nothing meself of politics an' such like, but she's a good, true woman, is Queen Victoria, with a woman's heart; for didn't I read with me own two eyes, as how she went to one of them soldiering hospitals, an' says she (God bless her for it!), 'Show me one of me brave, brave men, from Ireland.' An' the doctor, he takes her, smart enough, to

74

the bed where was spread one of our own Irish boys, what had seventeen wounds in his body, without a word of a lie. An' when he smiled at her, an' she saw how ill he was, sure, an' bless her for it, the good lady, the tears rolled down her cheeks – they did so, Miss Dewie. I read it in the paper meself, an' says I to meself, says I, 'No wonder the soldiers love her, for, with all her grandeur, hasn't she the nature and the feelings of a poor woman, the likes of meself?' Sure, but my heart loved her, when I read it, it did; an' 'tis the truth I'm telling, Miss – ma'am."

"I think, Hannah," Dewla returned, looking around the friendly old sitting room, "that I have not been so happy in a long time as I have been tonight, here, talking to you."

And Hannah laughed and protested, but Dewla could see she was very touched and pleased by her words. She breathed deeply of the scent of her home – wood polish and the warm spring earth outside – and felt comforted in a way she had not felt in a very, very long time.

Lady, dost thou not fear to stray.
So lone and lovely, through this dark way?
Are Erin's sons so good, or so cold,
As not to be tempted by woman or gold?

Sir Knight, I feet not the least alarm,
No son of Erin will offer me harm;
For though they love women and golden store,
Sir Knight! they love honor and virtue more.
                    -- Thomas Moore

CHAPTER IX

How sweet, how passing sweet, is solitude –
But grant me still a friend in my retreat,
Whom I may whisper, "Solitude is sweet."
                                    -- Cowper.

I tremble when I think
How much I love him,
but I turn away
From thinking of it,
just to love him more –
Indeed, I fear, too much.
                        -- Frances R. Havergal.

HOW quiet and peaceful Claisín seemed to Dewla. Early springtime had dawned upon the woods, and the trees were bursting into leaf. Stray wildflowers lifted their sweet heads shyly among the long, soft grass. And Dewla, as she wandered about, so happy to see the dear woodland paths, and hunting for her favorite wildflowers, felt a strange feeling at her heart.

She was at home again, the home so dear to her. Nothing was changed, everything just as she had left it –

the house, the grounds, the dear lake itself – and yet something was lacking.

It was not her father's absence, nor yet her cousin Charlie's. For neither of these did her lonely heart yearn as it did for Hugh.

Night and day, she thought of him. As she wandered happily below her beloved trees, or as she sat writing at her desk, the thrushes hopping along the ledge outside her window, he was never far from her mind. Surely, he must love her even a little, or he would not have troubled to send so many anxious inquiries.

Oh! If – if – only his mother's cruel words were false! How happy would she be!

"Even if I never look upon his face again," she said within her heart, "I shall not cease to love him. Oh, Hugh, my husband!"

Hannah watched her narrowly from day to day. Nothing escaped her old nurse's keen, kind eyes. If she chanced to speak of "the master," as she called Hugh, she noticed how the color came back upon Dewla's cheeks, and her eyes grew soft and tender. Sometimes a smile would play upon her lips at the mention of his name.

After one such episode, the old woman noticed Dewla's eyes glitter suddenly when she mentioned Hugh, and the girl quickly excused herself and left the room. She was certain that Dewla was trying to hide her tears. "Surely, something is wrong," Hannah thought. "There isn't no letter coming nor going from her – 'cept to editors – an' he don't know she's here, that's sure."

She frowned to herself. "Well, I don't care if they says I'm a troublesome old woman, but I'll send the master a little line, on the sly. I will! For I liked the looks of him mighty well, an' he can't help being English – 'twasn't no fault of his. He'd be Irish, I'll be bound, if he got the chance."

Smiling, she went to the little desk where she did up her accounts, and sat down, and picked up a quill. "So I'll send a line, I will, about Miss Dewie – I always forgets she's ma'am, I does. An' I won't tell no one."

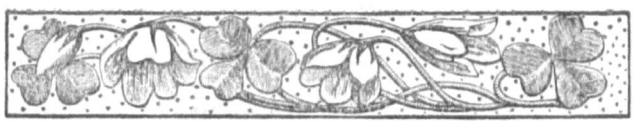

A laugh, which in the woodlands rang,
Bemocking April's gladdest bird,
A light and graceful form which sprang
To meet him when his steps were heard.
                    – Whittier.

It was a lovely evening, but tonight, Dewla felt unusually restless and oppressed. Hard though she tried to still the aching of her heart, she still grieved for Hugh.

Wandering out of doors, just as she used to do in the old, happy days, she turned her steps in the direction of the lonely lake. Only that morning, she had received the magazine containing her story, "Sunshine and Shadow." Would Hugh see and read it? Surely, he must recognize the signature, "Dewla." He had often told her he had never heard that name before.

Her heart thrilled as she wondered what he would think about the little tale.

As she stood now beside the low wall, which she had seen so plainly in her dream, she thought only of him – all else was blotted out and forgotten.

Instinctively, she shut her eyes, and, clasping her hands, prayed that God would bless him, now and always. This was ever the burden of her earnest petitions.

She stood thus in the softening light, the wide expanse of still, tranquil water lying at her feet, over which a stray kingfisher winged its homeward flight.

But then a sound fell upon her ears – the sound of an approaching footstep.

In wonder, she turned, to see whom the intruder might be, for none ever passed that way.

In a second, she recognized the advancing figure. It was Hugh.

In the suddenness of the meeting, joy triumphed over all her fears.

With a cry of delight, she ran towards him, and was clasped tightly in his strong, tender arms.

"Why did you leave me, Dewie?" Hugh asked as he held her fast, his voice broken with emotion.

"Because I loved you so well, that – that I fancied you would be happier when I was gone."

He did not speak for a moment. He seemed content to gaze upon her face, so beautiful now with its light of love stamped upon it.

"You overheard my mother talking with Miss Sedley?"

He asked the question gravely, and waited for an answer.

Dewla stirred in his tight embrace. "She is your mother, Hugh. I never did forget that fact, did I, dear?"

He kissed the tears from her eyes. "You are loyal to the core, Dewie – my Dewie! God grant that I may be more worthy of you in the future!"

"Why did you leave me, Dewie?"

They had much to say to each other. Sitting down upon the broken piece of wall, Dewla leaned her head upon his breast, and it seemed to her then that the happy vision of her dream had all come true.

For very joy, he could not speak – only sit and rest, his arms about her.

The sun had long sunk in the west, a peaceful stillness reigned around; one early star shone down upon them from out of the dark blue sky, yet they thought not of returning home.

"And so, my dear," Hugh was saying, with pitying gentleness, "you thought, because I knew you not in the delirium of fever, and spoke of Bella, that it was proof positive I loved not you, but her. Did you not know that, when people are so ill, they will say the most unlikely things, and even show dislike towards those they love best?"

Dewla shook her head. "I did not know," she faltered.

"That is not your fault," Hugh said gently. "It is mine. I should have paid more heed to your sadness, instead of laughing at you fears, and calling you a child."

These words brought the sudden tears to her eyes, and she lay her face against his chest.

"My lovely Dewie! You know not how I've suffered in those days that are past – days which will never come again. Yet the trial has done me good. It has shown me how precious was my sweet Kerry wife, and it strengthened my faith in mercy. To Him I cried in my hours of sorrow."

Dewla bowed her face upon the hands that clasped her own with a world of fondness in their grasp.

"Dewie," he whispered, "you cannot guess the joy poor old Hannah's ill-spelt letter brought to me – it made a new man of me. I shall always keep it, as a trophy, among my treasures."

Dewla raised her head in astonishment. "She told you I was here?"

"Oh, yes, but she only did because she was worried about you."

"And she never told me a word!" Dewla said, but there was no sign of regret in either face or voice.

"She knew her proud, young mistress better," he laughed. "Irish to the very letter, you would have forbidden her to send any word, eh, Dewie?"

"Possibly!" But her lips were all smiles.

The stars grew brighter, the earth and air more still, yet they heeded not the flight of time.

Thus old Hannah found them, for she had grown anxious at their long absence, and a little fearful as to the result of her self-imposed task.

"Sure, sir, I beg pardon, but I was in dread as how you'd gone and lost yourself, along with Miss Dewla – ma'am, I means. I always forgets myself, for it comes strange-like to me tongue, it do so! though I says it to meself often, to learn me a bit, but 'tis no use, your honor; I can't think of nothing 'cept Miss Dewla when I talks to her."

"Don't trouble, dear old nurse," answered her young mistress. "Any name sounds sweet, spoken by you."

"Thank you kindly, Miss D – ma'am," replied the old woman, highly pleased. "But sure, 'twas yourself was always thoughtful."

"Yes," Hugh said, standing and giving Dewla his hand. "You always have been."

Lives of good men all remind us
     We may make our lives sublime,
And, departing, leave behind us
     Footprints on the sands of time;

Footprints that perhaps another,
     Sailing o'er life's stormy main,
A forlorn and ship-wrecked brother,
     Seeing, may take heart again.
       -- Henry Wadsworth Longfellow

CHAPTER X

She stood by the western window,
In the mid-summer twilight fair;
And the sunset breeze leaped from the trees
To lift her wavy hair.

She glanced up quickly in my face,
Not sure that she heard aright;
And the shadow that fell in her sweet brown eyes,
Was sweeter than any light.
       – Frances R. Havergal.

NEITHER Dewla nor her husband appeared in any hurry to leave Claisín – both seemed more than happy in each other's company.

The country, too, was just beginning to look so lovely, it seemed a pity to even think of leaving the sunshine and the flowers behind. Hugh had been ordered rest and change; he was having both now. Dewla took him for walks to all her favorite old haunts, and the fresh air and exercise invigorated him. Daily he grew stronger, much to Dewla's satisfaction, who watched over him with all a wife's devotion and love.

Letters began arriving from Mrs. Jonathan and his sisters, and Dewla eyed them warily when she first saw them appearing on the breakfast table.

"They are demanding that I come home at once," Hugh said, reading the latest missive from his mother. Dewla could see that the pen had torn the paper in a few places, as if Mrs. Jonathan had been exceedingly wrathful when she wrote it.

Dewla felt the blood rush from her face. All speech gone, she shook her head in mute appeal.

Hugh set the letter aside, breaking into a smile. "My Dewie, my sweet spring flower," he said in words so warm that her heart melted. "I will never, never ask you to live again at Trafalgar House. Why, you are a completely different person here, so happy and contented. I saw a wren singing on her nest the other day, and it made me think of you, here in this grand old home of your ancestors."

Dewla covered her mouth, smiling as tears started to her eyes.

"I was wrong to have uprooted you and borne you away to my home," Hugh said, leaning back in his chair. "And every day, I must admit, this place grows on me a little more. Awfully far away from the club," he said wistfully. "On the other hand, I'd bet the hunting is good."

He had said this, and Dewla knew he meant it; therefore, she had no misgivings about the future. At last, her sky was blue and cloudless – all the darkness of doubt and sorrow was swept away.

Old Hannah rejoiced in secret over the joyful change in her dear mistress, and chuckled with delight to think that she had helped to bring it all about.

"How happy they looks, them two," she would mutter, peeping through the window and watching them strolling round the old shady garden, arm in arm. "It puts me in mind of a bit out of them stories Miss Dewla used to write when she was a bit of a child. Sure, but don't be talking – wasn't she always a wonder. An' the old master – rest his soul! – he was mighty proud of her. An' no wonder either, seeing there isn't her like nowhere!"

Then one morning, Dewla found an official-looking letter on the breakfast table, and her vision swam. Though it had been addressed to her, she pushed it to Hugh.

"What is this?" he asked.

"Open this for me," she said.

With a puzzled look, he opened the letter and perused the contents. Then he slowed in his reading and looked up at her, a shocked look in his face.

"Dewie," Hugh said, "I have sad tidings for you, poor girl."

"About Charlie?" she said, slowly, anxiously.

"Yes." He lay the letter down, smoothing it out on the table. "He died a noble, heroic death. You may well be proud of your kinsman."

Tears swam in her eyes, and trickled down her cheeks. "Poor Charlie!" she murmured. "In the old days, he used to say he'd like to die as his father had done, on the battlefield, fighting for his Sovereign and country."

"And so he has, poor chap! Here is the letter. His colonel speaks of him as being the bravest of the brave beloved by his fellow officers, and all who knew him, they one and all regretting deeply his early death, cut off in the flower of his youth. To a man, they beg to tender their deepest sympathy to you, his cousin."

"Poor Charlie!" said Dewla softly, brushing aside the tears as she read the letter. "He went away so proud and hopeful, full of vigor and courage. It seems so hard to think of him – dead – yet, surely, it is not death, Hugh, to pass from this troubled world to the endless life beyond. When dear father was taken from us, I used to try and think, not of his cold, still form lying in the tomb, but of the spirit, which God had glorified and taken to Himself into the glory land."

"Yes," returned Hugh, gravely. "Therein lies the great consolation of the Christian faith."

They were silent for a while. The sun shone though the old-fashioned window and rested upon Dewla's bent head, touching her brown hair with golden tints.

Hugh watched her, thinking all the while of how groundless had been his foolish suspicions – not so long ago, either.

"You cared for your cousin very much, Dewie?" he said suddenly.

She looked up, surprised somewhat at the abruptness of his question. "Why, of course! Charlie and I were as brother and sister, in the old days."

"And nothing more?"

He hardly knew why he put the question, knowing, in his secret heart, that there was no need to speak thus.

Again she lifted her head, not sure that she heard aright. "More?" she asked. "What do you mean by ..."

As the meaning of his words broke upon her, a shadow, soft and deep, crept into her sweet brown eyes.

"Oh, Hugh!" she almost sobbed. "You didn't – never for a moment have I ever thought that! Is that why you were so angry with me?"

Instantly his strong arms were about her, and he drew her closer to his breast.

"Please tell you didn't dream of such a thing, any more than I did," she went on, pleadingly.

Hugh hung his head. "My mother planted that suspicion in my mind," he confessed. "But I chose to believe her. I failed you, my dear Dewie."

Dewla shook her head helplessly. "Why, I used to be ashamed of myself often, when I remembered how little I thought of poor Charlie, even after he was wounded. My heart was so full of you – you only, Hugh – I seemed to have no room then for my poor, far-off cousin. Do you know that, though I received his very last letter" – with a catch in her breath— "the very morning of that Sunday I left Trafalgar House. Although I sat all breakfast-time with it before me, I could not read a

90

single word. The very lines swam before my eyes, and I seemed to see, instead of his penciled message, these words of my own: 'I am leaving Hugh today. After today, I may see my husband no more.' Poor Charlie's letter was of no interest to me, then. I could think of nothing but you, and the coming parting!"

There was the sound of tears in her voice. She would never speak of that terrible time without deep emotion.

A dull red color overspread Hugh's handsome face, as he bent and kissed the quivering lips of his fair, young wife. She looked up with a startled expression in her soft brown eyes.

"Dewie, I am unworthy of you, and your great love. I grow more ashamed of myself each day. Poor Charlie – he was worthier of you, a million times!"

Dewla raised her head to gaze into Hugh's eyes. "But you came to me when I needed you, and you chose to live here with me, in the land of my ancestors. Leave the past alone."

She nestled into his arms as they gazed out over the rolling estate, all green, its hallowed paths all edged with shamrocks.

With such love, purity, and valor, strong in the hearts of the sons and daughters of Erin's land, it is indeed small wonder that, today, you are the nation "whom the Queen delighteth to honor."

The End

Thus endeth the Shamrock Romances.

Don't stop here just because this particular series is over!

Skip on to the first episode of the next series, THE GUILTY BRIDEGROOM by Sydney Watson, a good old story from Victorian England, now tidied up and shaken into shape by our chipper Victorian book fiend and tireless editor, Eva Valentine.

You can find her on Twitter, posting from some workhouse in the English slums at @VictorianReader, or on Tumbler.

Keep up with the latest serials from merry England by subscribing to our newsletter, SERIALLY YOURS.

www.ingramcontent.com/pod-product-compliance
Lightning Source LLC
Chambersburg PA
CBHW030252270626
47156CB00021B/1748